To: David Allen II   2006

Love,

Papa and G̶̶̶ma Allen

Leprechaun Luck

A Wee Book of Irish Wisdom

by Erin Gobragh
Illustrated by Catharine O'Neill

Simon & Schuster Books for Young Readers

NEW YORK LONDON TORONTO SYDNEY SINGAPORE

SIMON & SCHUSTER BOOKS FOR YOUNG READERS • An imprint of Simon & Schuster
Children's Publishing Division • 1230 Avenue of the Americas, New York, New York 10020
Collection copyright © 2003 by Simon & Schuster, Inc. • Illustrations copyright © 2003 by
Catharine O'Neill • All rights reserved, including the right of reproduction in whole or in part in
any form. • SIMON & SCHUSTER BOOKS FOR YOUNG READERS is a trademark of Simon & Schuster.
Book design by Dan Potash • The text for this book is set in Gararond. • The illustrations for this
book are rendered in watercolor. • Manufactured in the United States of America

2 4 6 8 10 9 7 5 3 1

Library of Congress Cataloging-in-Publication Data • Leprechaun luck : a wee book of Irish wisdom /
[compiled] by Erin Gobragh; illustrated by Catharine O'Neill. • p. cm. • Summary:
A collection of Irish blessings, sayings, and verses about such things as friendship, home, and
happiness. • ISBN 0-689-85558-3 1. Ireland—Quotations, maxims, etc. 2. Quotations, English—
Ireland. • [1. Ireland—Quotations, maxims, etc. 2. Quotations.] I. Gobragh, Erin. II. O'Neill,
Catharine, ill. • PN6084.16 L47 2003
082'09417—dc21 • 2002005612

Walls for the wind,
And a roof for the rain,
And chairs beside the fire—
Laughter to cheer you
And those you love near you,
And all that your heart may desire!

Grant me a bit of humor, Lord,
The saving grace to see a joke,
To win some happiness from life,
And pass it on to other folks.

May you always walk in sunshine.
May you never want for more.
May Irish angels rest their wings right beside your door.

May your blessings outnumber
The shamrocks that grow.
And may trouble avoid you
Wherever you go.

May the saints protect ye
An' sorrow neglect ye.

May your troubles be as few and far apart as my grandmother's teeth.

May neighbors respect you,
Trouble neglect you,
The angels protect you,
And heaven accept you.

God bless the corners of this house,
And be the lintel blest,
And bless the heath and bless the board,
And bless each place of rest,
And bless each door that opens wide
To stranger as to kin,
And bless each crystal windowpane
That lets the starlight in,
And bless the rooftree overhead
And every sturdy wall.
The peace of man, the peace of God,
The peace of love on all.

As you slide down the banisters of life,
may the splinters never point the wrong way.

May the blessings
of each day
be the blessings
you need most.

May the embers from the open hearth warm your hands,
May the sun's rays from the Irish sky warm your face,
May the children's bright smiles warm your heart.

Deep peace of the running waves to you.
Deep peace of the flowing air to you.
Deep peace of the smiling stars to you.
Deep peace of the quiet earth to you.

May the wings of a butterfly kiss the sun
And find your shoulder to light on
To bring you luck, happiness, and riches
Today, tomorrow, and beyond.

May you be poor in misfortune,
Rich in blessings,
Slow to make enemies,
And quick to make friends,
But rich or poor, quick or slow,
May you know nothing but happiness
From this day forward.

May you enjoy the four greatest blessings:
Honest work to occupy you.
A hearty appetite to sustain you.
A good woman to love you.
And a wink from the God above.

May the lilt of Irish laughter
Lighten every load,
May the mist of Irish magic
Shorten every road.

If you find yourself on a stony path,
may you have strong shoes.

May the strength of three be in your journey.

May you have the hindsight to know where you've been,
the foresight to know where you're going.

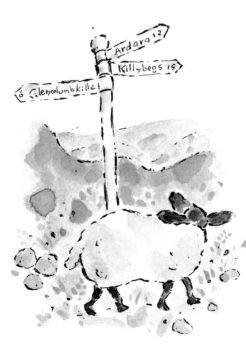

Wishing you joys that are lasting and true,
A heart that's not troubled or gray,
Friends who will travel life's pathway with you,
And the luck of the Irish each day.

Always remember to forget
The friends that proved untrue.
But never forget to remember
Those that have stuck by you.

May the blessing of light be on you—
light without and light within.
May the blessed sunlight shine on you
and warm your heart
till it glows like a great warm fire.

Wherever you go and whatever you do,
May the luck of the Irish be there with you.

May your right hand always be stretched out in friendship
and never in need.

May the blessing of the rain be on you—
the soft, sweet rain.
May it fall upon your spirit
so that all the little flowers
may spring up
and shed their sweetness on the air.
May the blessing of the great rains be on you,
may they beat upon your spirit
and wash it fair and clean,
and leave there many a shining pool
where the blue of heaven shines,
and sometimes a star.

May your
home always be too
small to hold all
of your friends.

May the hinges of our friendship never grow rusty.

May the first light of sun
Bless you.
When the long day is done
Bless you.
In your smiles and your tears
Bless you.
Through each day of your years
Bless you.

May you be blest
with the strength of heaven—
the light of the sun and the
radiance of the moon—
the splendor of fire—
the speed of lightning—
the swiftness of wind—
the depth of the sea—
the stability of earth and the firmness of rock.

May the Irish hills caress you.
May her lakes and rivers bless you.
May the luck of the Irish enfold you.
May the blessings of Saint Patrick behold you.

May there always be work for your hands to do;
May your purse always hold a coin or two;
May the sun always shine on your windowpane;
May a rainbow be certain to follow each rain;
May the hand of a friend always be near you;
May God fill your heart with gladness to cheer you.

May your pockets be heavy—
Your heart be light—
And may good luck pursue you
Each morning and night.

May you live as long as you want,
And never want as long as you live.

Bless you and yours
As well as the cottage you live in.

May you have warm words on a cold evening,
a full moon on a dark night,
and the road downhill all the way to your door.

Like the gold of the sun,
Like the light of the day,
May the luck of the Irish
Shine bright on your way—
Like the glow of a star
And the lilt of a song,
May these be your joys
All your life long.

Dance as if no one were watching,
Sing as if no one were listening,
And live every day as if it were your first.

May the road rise to meet you.
May the wind be always at your back.
May the sun shine warm upon your face
And rains fall soft upon your fields.
And until we meet again,
May God hold you in the hollow of His hand.